The Adventures of Harley, the Sugar Glider

Author: Christie Drawdy

Illustrations by: Cindy Surin

PAGE PUBLISHING, INC.
New York, NY

First originally published by Page Publishing, Inc. 2015

ISBN 978-1-68139-802-0 (pbk)
ISBN 978-1-68139-803-7 (digital)

Printed in the United States of America

Special thanks to Nana, Poppy, and Alan for helping in the search and family and friends for your encouragement.

Hi, my name is Harley. I'm a sugar glider. You might think I am a flying squirrel, but I'm not. I am a nocturnal marsupial. That means I am awake at night, and my birth mother has a pouch on her belly for me to sleep in.

When I was eight weeks old, I went to the county fair. Boy, was that a big day for me! I got to smell all sorts of new things like elephants, tigers, donkeys, pigs, horses, and even a llama. I also smelled many different foods from the concession stands that sold hamburgers, hot dogs, cotton candy, candy apples, and sugary drinks. I saw lots of carnival rides like the Ferris Wheel, House of Mirrors, and a Tilt-a-World too.

I thought I was going to the fair just to have fun, but it turned out that it was also where and when I was adopted by my human parents. I was put into a comfortable blue pouch with an apple slice inside. Then my new daddy wore me on his chest, so I could get used to his smell. At first, I screamed a lot! I was scared! But Daddy held me tight, and then I felt secure and safe. I also met my new mommy, nana, and poppy. They all took turns holding me in my pouch, so I could learn their smells too.

We left the fair and went straight to an apple festival. My new family bought me fresh apples and apple juice because they are my favorites. Turns out apples are also very, very healthy for me.

Daddy and Mommy set up my new cage and dining room when we got home. They gave me some of the fresh apple juice. Boy, was that good stuff! I got to meet my sister, brother, and cousins. I'm a little confused because they're dogs and cats. I think they were a little confused too, because they kept coming up to my cage and trying to smell me to figure me out.

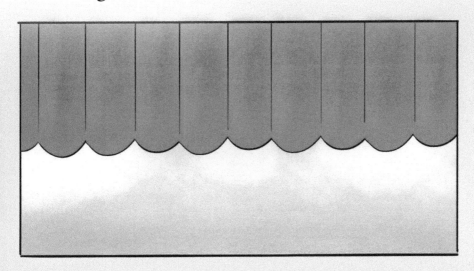

The first week with my new family, I had to stay in the pouch when someone wanted to hold me. This made me feel secure and helped me get familiar with my new family's smells. I learned their smells quickly and was able to be held in one of my daddy's shirts after that. I became very curious and adventurous. I wanted to investigate everything!

That's when I thought I would explore the outdoors. Little did I know, this was *not* safe. I remember that morning so well. Daddy was letting the doggies out to go potty. I was curious to see where they went, so I jumped off Daddy's hands, and off I went. It was still dark outside, so I could see really well. Daddy started calling my name, but I was too interested in exploring the outside world. I was running and jumping all over the place. Then I started hearing Mommy calling me along with Daddy. But this was too much fun. I figured if the doggies can go outside, so can I.

I noticed they had a big backyard full of
huge trees with acorns and pecans on
them. That's when I met Ms. Cardinal.
She was sitting in her nest on three
eggs. She asked, "Who are you?"

"My name is Harley," I
replied.

Then she asked, "What
are you? I've never seen
anyone like you before."

I said, "I'm a sugar glider. I like playing at night."

"You had better get back home then because it is almost time for
the sun to come up," Ms. Cardinal said.

So I asked, "Can I just curl up in your nest for the day?"

"Oh no, sweetheart. I don't have any room. Wish I could help.
Good luck finding some place to sleep," answered Ms. Cardinal as
she waved good-bye.

Then I heard Nana's and Poppy's voices along with Mommy's voice calling me back home, but I couldn't see them. You see, I can't see well when the sun is out. Plus, I get very tired during the day. So I figured I'd go to sleep. That way, when I woke up, it would be dark because it would be nighttime. Then I could start exploring again. So I found a little notch in the tree, curled up, and fell asleep.

Then I woke up. Boy, was I cold and hungry. I looked out from the tree and I saw another sugar glider. So I ran down the tree and over to him.

I said, "Hi, I didn't know there were other sugar gliders around here."

"Are you talking to me? I'm not a sugar glider. I'm a chipmunk," replied Charlie.

I said, "I'm sorry. Now that I'm closer, I can see you are bigger than I am. So you live around here?"

"I sure do. I was just about to go find dinner," answered Charlie.

"Find dinner? You mean your mommy and daddy don't bring dinner to you?" I asked.

"No, my mom hasn't brought me dinner since I was six months old. If you're hungry, follow me. I'll show you how it's done in the wild," Charlie said.

Off we went running through the yard, finding acorns. I was thankful he helped me find food. It was good. But I have to admit, I like the food Mommy and Daddy gave me better.

Once I was full, I wanted to explore the backyard some more. I thanked Charlie Chipmunk for the wonderful dinner and told him I was going to check out the yard.

He warned me, "Just remember, not everyone is friendly like me. Be careful of the snakes and owls."

I wasn't sure what a snake or owl looked like, but I told him I'd be careful. Then off I went.

I went running in the bushes, up more trees, through pipes under the porch, and in the rocks. Even though it was getting cold, I was having a blast. That's when I almost met Jake. He looked weird. He didn't have any legs. He also slid on his belly. Thank God, Suzie Squirrel jumped out of the tree and stopped me from going over to Jake.

She said, "Are you crazy? Don't you know who that is?"

"No, who is it?" I asked.

"That's Jake the Snake! He will eat you!" Suzie exclaimed.

I said, "Eat *me*! What do you mean eat me?"

"Boy, don't you know anything? He's a snake. They eat animals like us," she said.

So I thanked her for stopping me and saving my life. Then I ran as fast as I could in the opposite direction. I thought, maybe the wild isn't that great. But then I thought I would play some more, just way far away from Jake the Snake's house.

I was running through the grass when I heard a swoosh over my head. I ducked into a bush. Suddenly, Charlie Chipmunk came out of nowhere and into the bush with me.

He said, "I thought I told you to watch out for snakes and owls?"

"You did, but I didn't know what they looked like. But, boy, do I know now. I don't like living in the wild. I miss my family. I want to go home! Can you help me?" I cried.

"Sure. Follow me. I'll get you back to the porch and then the rest is up to you," Charlie answered.

We jumped from bush to bush to stay out of the owl's sight. We finally made it back to the porch. I thanked Charlie for his help and said good-bye. I made it up the stairs, and to my surprise, my family was all standing there, waiting for me to come home. I jumped into Daddy's hands, and he wrapped me up in a blanket. Mommy gave me an apple and some yogurt. Boy, was I happy to be home!

The End

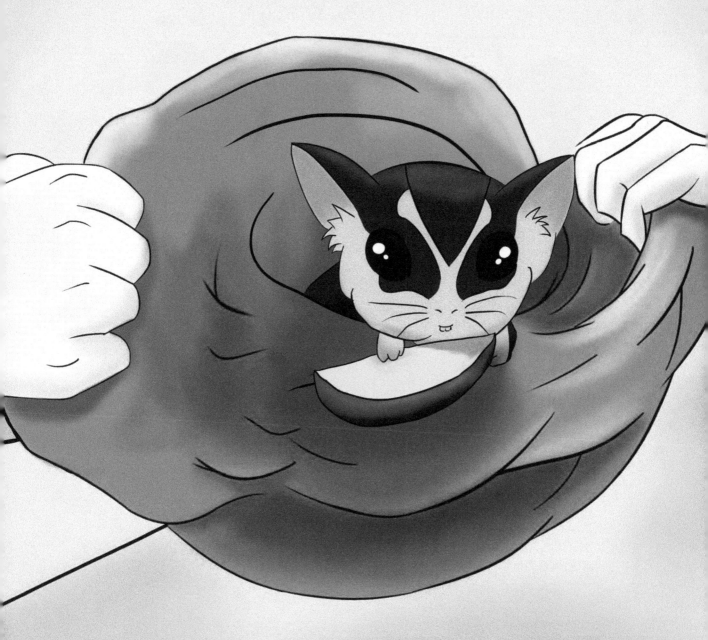

About the Author

Christie Drawdy is a wife, mother of two, and a speech language pathologist. In 1973, she was born to her wonderful parents in Naperville, Illinois. Her family moved to Florida when she was nine. While in Florida, she graduated from the University of Central Florida with a BS and MA in communicative disorders. During that time, she met and married her husband, Dennis. She has worked as a speech language pathologist since 1995. Her primary workplace has been in schools, but she has also worked in hospitals and home health care. She enjoys working with children. She currently lives in South Carolina with her family.

Writing this book was unexpected and exciting, particularly because she was able to work with her mom, who illustrated this book. She looks forward to continuing this collaboration in the future.

CPSIA information can be obtained
at www.ICGtesting.com
Printed in the USA
BVHW052143011020
590082BV00002B/28